Turtle's Pond

A SENECA FOLKTALE

Written by Karen Sharp Foster
Illustrated by Bruce Martin

The warm days had grown cool.

The alder leaves had turned orange and red.

Turtle yawned a long autumn yawn.

It was time for the sleep of winter.

He looked around his beautiful home.

Trees sprang out of the grassy carpet around his pond.

Wildflowers lined the muddy banks

where he had spent long summer days napping in the sun.

A tiny brook trickled into one end of his pond

and out the other.

Turtle took a deep breath.

Then he paddled to the bottom of the pond.

He burrowed into the soft,

oozy mud and went to sleep.

Soon a newcomer came to the pond.

"What a beautiful place!" he said.

"I think I will live here!"

He cut down the alder trees and dragged them into the pond.

He piled them high to make a dam

so the water could not trickle out.

Before long, water covered all the oozy mud.
It covered the wildflowers and the grass.
It covered most of the stumps where the
alder trees had been.
The newcomer made his home under
another pile of logs.
He crawled inside and he, too, went to sleep.

In the spring Turtle woke up. He paddled toward the top of the water. But the top was not where he had left it! Higher and higher he paddled. At last he burst out of the water, gasping for breath. "Where are the alder trees?" he said. "Where are the flowers? Where is the oozy mud? What has happened to my beautiful pond?"

"Your pond?" said a voice behind him. It was Beaver.

"This is my pond. I have made my home here.

You will have to leave."

"This is not your home!" said Turtle.

"I was here first! It is you who must leave!"

"I will not!" said Beaver.

"And I will not!" said Turtle.

“Then we must have a contest,” said Beaver.

“The one who loses must leave.”

“A contest it will be, then,” said Turtle.

The two agreed to have a race across the pond.

Beaver knew he would win with his strong, broad tail.

Turtle was a good swimmer, too, but he was small.
He would have to swim very hard to win.
The race began.
The two shot like arrows through the water, swimming with all their might.

As they neared the far bank, Turtle began to get tired.

What if he lost the race?

What if he had to leave his home forever?

Beaver swam past flapping his strong, broad tail.

Suddenly Turtle had an idea.

As the tail flipped past his face,

Turtle grabbed the end of it in his mouth and hung on.

The skin on Beaver's tail was thick.

He could not feel Turtle's bite, but his tail did feel heavier.

Beaver's swimming slowed.

"I'm just getting tired," he thought.

The bank was close.

He looked around, but he could not see Turtle.

“Ah, good!” he said. “Turtle has fallen behind!

I am sure to win!”

He gave his tail one last flip to gain speed.

The flip sent Turtle flying through the air.

THUMP! Turtle landed on the bank just ahead of Beaver.

“What?” exclaimed Beaver. “How did you get here so fast?” Turtle smiled. “Please remove the logs before you go, Beaver,” he said.

Turtle's pond is the most beautiful place in the world.

Alder seedlings grow from the grassy carpet around the pond.

Wildflowers line the muddy banks.

Look carefully at the squishy mud.

You will see a happy little turtle, napping in the sun.